D1602889

The theme running through CALL ME BANDICOOT is stinginess. The story is one of a series of books by the author on the seven deadly sins. LAZY TOMMY PUMPKINHEAD is a book about sloth. PRETTY PRETTY PEGGY MOFFITT treats vanity with appropriate style, and PORKO VON POPBUTTON is bursting with gluttony.

"Well, one day it was sunglasses."

WILLIAM PENE DU BOIS

CALL ME
BANDICOOT

HARPER & ROW, PUBLISHERS
New York, Evanston, and London

CALL ME
BANDICOOT

I was dazzled by a pair of the brightest eyes I'd ever seen.

The ferryboat from Manhattan to Staten Island slaps, splashes, and grumbles through New York harbor straight as an arrow through a valentine heart. I was once aboard, leaning on the rail, deep in thoughts of no importance, when I overheard a boy's voice to starboard, below my right ear, announce, "Filthy, isn't it?"

I'm not an easy collector of friends, and as I switched on the cold face I use to cut short palsy-walsy chitchat, I was dazzled by a pair of the brightest eyes I'd ever seen. An odd-thinking psychologist once wrote that only children with a light in their eyes are worth sending to school. If bright eyes do reflect bright minds, I thought

7

it would be wrong to cut short the ideas of this young genius.

"What?" I asked stupidly.

"What what?" he countered.

"What's filthy?"

"Why the water, of course. Isn't that what you were looking at?"

"I suppose I was," I muttered.

"Scoop out a glass of the stuff, hold it up to the light, and what do you suppose you would find?" asked the kid.

"Visible or invisible?"

"Visible."

"Well, it would be brownish in color, and flaked with bits of brown stuff not unlike tobacco."

"Right," said the kid. "Dead on the nose. It *is* tobacco—most of it. Ever heard of a boy named Ermine Bandicoot?"

I was slightly staggered by the silliness of the name. "Ermine Bandicoot? I can't say that I have."

"His work," said the kid, pointing to the water below, "all his foul work."

"He must smoke up a storm," I offered.

"Ermine Bandicoot doesn't smoke at all," said the boy, "too stingy. He only eats free meals. Breathes a lot though. He's the stingiest, money-grubbingest cat that ever was." The kid gave me

8

a sly do-you-want-to-hear-more look which I was first tempted to resist. Alas, I was trapped by my own curiosity.

"OK, Buster," I sighed, "tell me how Ermine Bandicoot filled New York harbor with tobacco."

"It will cost you a hot dog and soda pop in the lounge," said the kid. He had the nerve to head in that direction—and I followed.

The snack bar in the lounge of a Staten Island ferryboat is a square construction, staffed by three sturdy ladies. They wear white uniforms which look like tough tests in TV laundry-soap commercials: squashed-in coffee spots, pounded-in body dirt, bashed-in mustard. As I approached, I thought I heard one of them say, "The weasel's caught another fish," but it didn't mean much to me at the time. The kid ordered in sign language and picked the longest hot dog with everything free piled on high. He got a soda pop of unknown brand which came in a large bottle. I paid the ransom, and we sat near the window on the Statue of Liberty side of the boat.

"I live in New York City and go to school in Staten Island with Ermine Bandicoot," the boy started. "He looks ratlike, as his name suggests. His forehead slopes down to his nose, and his nose slopes down to his Adam's apple. Somewhere

9

along the way, he has a mouth which opens rather wide." As he said this, his own mouth opened wide enough to admit roll, hot dog, mustard, ketchup, kraut, pickles, and onions. His upper incisors were longer than his other teeth, and they gnawed through the mess neatly, wasting nothing. "You might say his style of dress is buttoned-down," he added, spraying crumbs as he spoke.

"What does that mean?" I asked.

Before answering he took another bite, ballooning his cheeks. "Well, everything is skintight and fastened down. His skimpy suit has four buttons down the front and three on each cuff. His shirts have button-down collars, and a tab which buttons shirt to trousers. His shirt cuffs are double-buttoned. His skinny tie is clipped to his shirt and pinned down with an old brass horseshoe he got in a Cracker Jack box. His socks are gartered to his skinny legs, and his boots are buckled to his ankles. He wears both a belt and suspenders. His trouser pockets have zippers." He paused for a gassy swill of pop. He stood up, as though to catch a better look at a passing freighter, and I noticed that he might have been describing himself. Face, suit, shoes, buttons, buckles, zippers— all fit the description right down to the brass horseshoe pinning his tie. I thought this odd, but

I noticed that he might have been describing himself.

then some kids are style-setters. Friends of Ermine Bandicoot might well copy Ermine Bandicoot, just as friends of Beethoven, Buffalo Bill, and the Beatles might well wear long hair and crazy suits.

"How did he get to be so stingy?" I asked. "Was he born that way?"

"Not at all," said the kid curtly.

"Then how?" I repeated.

"I could sure use another hot dog," was his answer.

"It's cost me fifty-five cents to find out how Ermine Bandicoot looks and dresses," said I. "How much will it cost to hear how he got all that tobacco into New York harbor?"

The kid looked away. "This is a short ferryboat ride," said he, strumming his skinny fingers on the bench. "Time's awastin'." He looked off to sea, sighed, then shut his eyes as if to take a nap. I could see that to get him to tell the story, I would have to refuel him regularly. It was insane, but nonetheless I found myself giving him the thirty cents.

He was off and back at the bench in a matter of seconds. He screwed up his face and talked out of the side of his mouth. "Ah, yes," said he. "How did Ermine Bandicoot get to be so stingy? Good question . . ."

12

"Never mind the W. C. Fields impersonation," I interrupted. "Get on with your story."

"It's the same price," he said. "However, be that as it may, it was on a Fourth of July, seven, eight, or nine years ago. Ermine Bandicoot was a mere child of seven. At that time he and his family lived on a country farm, deep in the lush hills and woods of Staten Island. There was a sound of firecrackers in the air, the rapid-fire little ones popping gaily, with the loud banging salutes and cherry bombs. A warm sea breeze mixed its sweet air with the acrid smell of gunpowder and punk. Young Ermine Bandicoot walked into the living room and said, 'Pop, give me three dollars.'

" 'What?' his old man barked.

" 'Please?' the twerp asked sweetly.

" 'Give you three dollars?' asked the father.

" 'I knew you heard me the first time,' said young Ermine. He then tried to win his dad with childish giggles.

" 'What for?' the father asked.

"Now the father was king-sized, you know, huge and puffy. He was lying in a real barber chair he had bought for himself as a gift. The chair raised his legs, lowered his head, bent him, folded him, or stretched him out flat—just by pumping handles. He was planted in front of a

"*. . . as a bizarre added touch, two rearview motorcycle mirrors.*"

remote-control color television set, watching his favorite baseball club get clobbered in a Fourth of July doubleheader. He was smoking king-sized cigarettes, and under his right hand, within easy reach, was a red fire bucket, full of ice and quart-size beer cans. A huge ashtray was built into the left arm of the chair that also possessed, as a bizarre added touch, two rearview motorcycle mirrors. 'Three dollars. What for?' he repeated.

"'Firecrackers.'

"'Firecrackers!' the old man exploded. He pumped handles madly until his chair folded him in an upright position and spun him around to face little Ermine. 'Come here, son, I want to tell you something.'

"'Boy, oh boy,' thought young Bandicoot.

"Old Pop Bandicoot took young Ermine's skinny upper arms in his fat hands, looked him straight in the eyes, and said, 'Son, do you know what shooting off firecrackers is?'

"'I guess so,' said Ermine. He'd shot his piggy-bank's worth that morning.

"'No, you don't,' said Pop Bandicoot.

"'What is shooting off firecrackers?' Ermine Bandicoot asked.

"'Shooting off firecrackers is nothing more nor less than burning money. Get it? Burning money!

You might just as well take a bag of gunpowder and a bunch of dollar bills, roll them into cigars, and blow them up. Get the picture? Shooting off firecrackers is just BURNING MONEY!'

"Before Ermine Bandicoot could say anything, something happened which changed his whole life. The kitchen door swung open and Mom Bandicoot burst into the room. 'Listen to who talks about burning money!' she shouted. She walked over to Pop Bandicoot, yanked the cigarette from his mouth, shook it in his face, and said, 'Just what do you think smoking cigarettes is?' She stalked up and down the living room. 'You might just as well take a bunch of dollar bills, shred them up, roll 'em in squares of toilet paper—and smoke 'em!' She stalked some more. 'It would be better for your health than tobacco, and just about as cheap!' She stomped back into the kitchen and lit the oven with a bang.

"'Can't a guy watch a ball game on the Fourth of July?' Pop Bandicoot asked, pumping himself back into viewing position. 'Everybody out!' he shrieked."

"How did all that change Ermine Bandicoot?" I asked.

"It was D-Day in his life," the kid said. "Decision Day. It is a rare day when something parents

say really gets through to a kid. Ermine Bandicoot
was struck right between the eyes. From listening
to his parents shout, he decided money must be
everything. Then Ermine Bandicoot made one of
those big discoveries that only little guys make.
A huge piece of idiot thinking. It went something
like this. Shooting off firecrackers is like burning
money, but there is no money in shot firecrackers.
All that's left is smelly burnt cardboard and pink
tissue paper. Smoking cigarettes is like burning
money, but almost half of any cigarette is thrown
away unfinished. Since cigarettes are like money,
Ermine Bandicoot decided to save butts and make
a million! Shivers of glory ran up and down his
backbone. Come to think of it, not too long ago
he made it pay off," said the kid wistfully.

"How?"

"Long about now, an apple turnover à la mode
would go great," the kid answered. He strummed
his bony fingers on the table. "Heavy on the
mode." He stared at the filthy harbor water which
sparkled from the sun's reflection. "Another pop
wouldn't hurt either," he added, gargling bottle-
bottom dregs through a straw.

He had me hooked. I can't imagine why, but
I felt I just had to find out how Ermine Bandicoot
made cigarette butts pay off. I paid the kid off,

17

and he left and returned with an apple turnover, ice cream, and pop.

"Ermine Bandicoot started collecting butts. At first he was slow, but when you put your entire effort into one project, you soon get to be expert. He started off in gutters. No good. It's piecework. But there are side rewards. His eyes sharpened, and he started finding coins. These coins to him were pure gold, his capital. Then the kid discovered parties. Every time he went to a party where kids and parents were invited, he'd run around emptying ashtrays into a shopping bag. The parents thought he was a great little helper. The kids thought he was nuts.

"He got to hanging around hotels where they have big parties, such as wedding receptions, and sneaking in with his shopping bags. He looks sort of like anybody's relative, and he got away with it every time. They were a gold mine in butts.

"He weaseled his way into political conventions, hung around the halls until the big bosses piled out of their smoke-filled rooms, then—"

"What a grubby life," I interrupted.

"Yes. He was fast turning into a rotten little miser—sort of like his name, Ermine Bandicoot. An ermine is a weasel who turns white in winter to blend with the snow, just like he blended with the crowd at a party, uninvited. A bandicoot comes in two kinds, the East Indian variety, which is a big rat, and the Australian variety, which has a little pocket. He got to be like that, a rat running around unobserved all day, stuffing butts in his pocket."

"What was Ermine Bandicoot like in school?" I quickly asked, before the kid finished his pop and turnover.

"A moneylender. All kids at school spend a great deal of time borrowing money from each other. Ermine Bandicoot had this money he'd find while looking for butts, his capital, and he lent it, but made you sign a little contract. For every dollar you borrowed, you had a choice of paying him back one dollar and ten cents, or one dollar plus one half hour of labor any time he needed you. Most kids charge interest. The problem is finding one with loot who lends. The kids always chose the labor because for a long time Ermine Bandicoot never asked anyone to do anything."

"Where did he keep his collection?"

"Well, at first, when he thought he'd made such a red hot discovery, he tried to keep it secret. He squeezed his clothes from his bottom drawers into his top drawers and filled the bottom drawers with butts. He threw away his toys and filled his toy chest with butts. He filled a closet in the maid's room—the Bandicoots had no maid—filled her bathroom, stuffed the whole maid's room, top to bottom. Things like that. Of course, somewhere along the line, Mom and Pop Bandicoot discovered their son's secret. Ermine Bandicoot doesn't know when, but somewhere along the line there must have been a serious little talk between Mom and Pop about how the kid had changed since that Fourth of July, how he never asked for money anymore, what a little whiz at arithmetic their darling had become, how neatly he dressed—he had to look well to crash parties—things like that. They could see little harm in butt-collecting. This is the Age of Aquarius. Every family has some kind of nut, and theirs didn't even smoke." He paused in his story to eye the food counter again.

"May we get to the tobacco in New York harbor?" I asked, handing him a dollar bill.

"How nice," said he. He sprinted to the counter and returned with a fistful of candy bars. "But, of course, it is nicer to give than to receive." He gave me my change one coin at a time, as if each were a reward.

"Prove it," said I.

"Prove what?"

"That it is nicer to give than to receive."

20

"Nothing could be simpler," said the kid. He scanned the horizon. "Take the Statue of Liberty out there. The French people chipped in two hundred and fifty thousand dollars to make it, took it apart, packed it in two hundred wooden cases, and sent it as a gift to the American people, without a pedestal. The American people had to chip in two hundred and eighty thousand dollars to put her back together and build a pedestal for her. Moral: It is thirty thousand dollars nicer to give than to receive."

"How do you know so much about the Statue?" I asked.

"Ermine Bandicoot again," the kid said. "He's a nut on the subject. You see, we live in Manhattan and go to school in Staten Island. We take this same ride back and forth every day. Come on out on deck," he shouted. He left, and I followed meekly. He pointed at the Statue of Liberty. "The Copper Goddess, he calls her. He's figured out more uses for her than there are days in a year. He comes up with a new use every trip."

"Uses for the Statue of Liberty?" I asked.

"Uses," said the kid. "Ermine Bandicoot thinks the Statue of Liberty is the greatest advertising triumph in history. She's the trademark for the whole United States. But he thinks her invitation

"He filled a closet in the maid's room, filled her bathroom."

was received, the guests came, the party's over, time to dim the lamp."

"What invitation?"

"Why, the poem on her pedestal"—the kid struck a ham-actor pose—"you know:

Keep, ancient lands, your storied pomp!...
Give me your tired, your poor,
Your huddled masses yearning to breathe free,
The wretched refuse of your teeming shore.
Send these, the homeless, tempest-tost, to me,
I lift my lamp beside the golden door!"

He bowed to a scattering of applause from other passengers.

"You see," he continued, "they came. So many huddled masses squeezed into New York City they had to be piled on top of each other in skyscrapers. The poor, tired, tempest-tost, and homeless swamp the welfare rolls. The wretched refuse clogs the gutters. 'Dim the lamp,' says Ermine Bandicoot, 'at least until the mess can be straightened out.'"

"What would *he* do with the Statue of Liberty?" I asked, though I somehow dreaded the answer.

"Well, one day it was sunglasses," the kid said. He looked out to sea.

"Sunglasses?"

24

"Yes, of course. It was a day like today. The sun was bouncing off the harbor and smacking the Copper Goddess in the eyes. Ermine Bandicoot looked at her and said, 'You know her face is over ten feet wide, cheekbone to cheekbone—more, counting her hair. Each eye is over two and a half feet wide. Give her twelve-foot sunglasses with five-foot lenses. Put the maker's name in lights on the pedestal. She'd sell a million pairs a day!'"

"Good grief!"

"One late afternoon in autumn," the kid continued, "the days were shorter, and it was getting dark. Ermine Bandicoot looked at the Statue of Liberty and said, 'Put giant hair-curlers on the spikes of her crown, then cover them over with a huge nightcap. Put a great candle where the torch is, and there you would have it—the lady is off to bed in her nightgown, with a best seller in her left hand. Put the name of the best seller in lights on the pedestal blinking on and off. She'd sell a million copies!'"

The kid paused, seemed to study my reaction, then continued, "He was really hung up on the nightgown idea. Ermine Bandicoot once said, 'She's supposed to be holding the Declaration of Independence in that left arm, but it looks more like the Sunday edition of *The New York Times*.

" 'Put a steaming cup of coffee in her right hand.' "

Put a steaming cup of
coffee in her right hand.
Run the news around her
pedestal in electric lights,
and circulation would double.
Everyone knows how ladies like
to sit around in their nightgowns
and curlers Sunday mornings, read-
ing *The New York Times.'* Then, of
course, news stories always gave him
ideas.''

"What? For example?"

"Well, the day after the moon landing he
looked at her and said, 'The Copper Goddess
has a steel structure inside, which weighs two

26

hundred and twenty-five tons. She's strong. It was made by Eiffel, the man who built the tower. It's hard to see her feet from below, but they have broken shackles at the ends of the chains attached to her ankles. She broke those shackles herself.

That's how she got to be Miss Liberty. They're making whopping big rockets these days. Why not put the Copper Goddess in orbit? Her crown alone has seven nose cones. What a plug for America! Miss Liberty, free from friction, free from gravity, free and orbiting the world for all to see, her chains and broken shackles a flying inspiration. Hope in orbit. Think of the lonely American soldier in some pesthole far from home. Once an hour this familiar free lady would fly over him, a sweet touch of home to lighten his day, brighten his night—'"

"About that tobacco in New York harbor?" I interrupted.

"Partly her fault," said the kid.

"The Statue of Liberty's fault?" I asked.

"Right. A few months ago there were two campaigns in New York newspapers, one was against air pollution, the other against smoking cigarettes."

"Both campaigns are still going strong," I offered.

"Yes, of course," said the kid. "Great campaigns. Ermine Bandicoot thought no one could handle the mess better than he and the Statue of Liberty. His idea was to roll his entire butt collection into one cigarette just a bit taller than the statue, then stand it on end next to the statue. You must admit it would be an eye-catcher. Then, with the wind blowing into New York City, light the mammoth cigarette. I know you've smelled a butt burning in an ashtray. Foul, isn't it? All of New York would soon be coughing, choking, and gagging from one huge burning butt. In no time both the air-pollution and cigarette-smoking campaigns would get all the attention they could possibly ask for."

"But where does the Statue of Liberty fit into this?" I asked. I had lost his attention. He was watching a man who had just had his shoes shined poking a finger through a whole fistful of change. Sure enough, a nickel fell out and rolled across the deck, in and out of the shallow gutter which edges the deck, and out over the harbor. The kid leapt like a cat, thrust a quick hand through the rails, and snatched the five-cent piece in midair. He zipped open a trouser pocket, slid it in, patted it a few whacks to help it join and jingle with its new mates, and sat back down next to me.

"Aha," said he, "the Statue of Liberty. Where does she—"

He was interrupted by the man with the shiny shoes. "I say," he said pleasantly, "that's my nickel you've caught there."

The kid slowly stood up, slowly turned to the

man, gave him an icy stare, and muttered through gritting teeth, "Any fool knows that, at sea, a coin caught in midair belongs to the catcher!" He pulled his skinny jacket down, pulled his trouser legs up, sat down, and slowly turned to me.

The man appeared stunned at first, then, stuttering, mumbled, "This *fool* doesn't know anything of the kind, why I—"

"Well, you know it now!" shouted the kid. He turned to me, "As I was saying—"

"For goodness sake," I whispered, "give the gentleman back his five-cent piece."

He gave me the same icy stare. "Why don't *you* call the captain?" he screamed. The man with the shiny shoes shrugged his shoulders, stood up, and walked away grunting. I remember having the rotten feeling that he might think the brat was my boy.

"Aha," the kid continued, as though nothing had happened, "people hate to be told what they can or cannot do. The Statue of Liberty means freedom to live and act as you please. Ermine Bandicoot would need help in standing his cigarette next to the statue. He thought of getting a cigarette company to pay for the job. People were being told not to smoke. He thought that his huge cigarette, towering over the Statue of Liberty, would carry a clear message, such as SMOKE ALL YOU WANT! SEND ME YOUR PUFFERS, DRAGGERS, INHALERS, etc. Then too, the statue would look like a whopping cigarette lighter, and what an audience it would get! The skyscrapers overlooking the harbor are one big beehive of tycoons!"

"But I thought you said he planned to light the cigarette and stink up New York City."

"Yes, of course. But he wasn't going to tell that to the cigarette company. All he would tell them was that their cigarette would tower over the Statue of Liberty, in plain view of New York City's choicest audience."

"Did the cigarette company agree?"

"They loved the idea, but wanted first to see the cigarette. Then too, there was a lot of talk about permission to erect such a monument on city property. Ermine Bandicoot went to see the Mayor and had no trouble getting an interview. The Mayor was fascinated by his silly name. He just *had* to see the face that went with it. Ermine Bandicoot was ushered right into his office. He was at his best. He told the Mayor that his plan would give the anti-pollution and anti-cigarette campaigns enormous free publicity at the stroke of a match. He was running all over the office, performing in pantomime. Pretending he was the Mayor, he climbed an imaginary ladder, lit a huge imaginary match, struck heroic poses, made a speech, posed for news and television cameras, slid down the ladder, took a bow. The Mayor loved the idea, but wanted first to see the cigarette."

"I thought you said Ermine Bandicoot made cigarette-butt collecting pay off. So far, I see little money coming for years of effort, and a rotten stingy life."

For the first time the lad's face looked sad and gentle. Then it brightened and hardened. "Postcards!" he shouted. "Ermine Bandicoot made a small fortune selling postcards."

"I can't see much money in that," I offered.

"I told you he traveled back and forth to school on this ferry, didn't I? While the cigarette was up, he ran up and down the decks, selling souvenir postcards to passengers. Everybody bought 'em. Here, do you want some?" He pulled out one each of two cards from his jacket side pockets and whizzed them past my eyes, too fast to study. I think I saw a huge fuzzy cigarette, slightly taller than the statue it stood by. "How many do you want?"

I didn't answer right off. I didn't want any.

"The colored one is twenty-five cents, and the

black and white is fifteen cents. How many do you want?" the kid repeated.

"They seem expensive," said I.

"They're exclusive!" he shouted. "Collectors' items."

"I don't collect postcards," I said. Then, thinking they would make a souvenir of this ridiculous ride, I added, "I suppose I'll take one of each."

"Only one?"

"Well, one of each."

"Why not take two colored ones?"

"One of each," I repeated.

"Oh," said he. He placed them in a cheap brown envelope, swiftly licked it, and pounded it shut. He handed it to me in the same motion with which I handed him a dollar. He turned his back to me and bent over for privacy while he reached into his jacket and zipped open an inside pocket. It seems his wallet was top secret. He put my dollar away. He zipped open a trouser pocket, fingered around, then gingerly eased out a quarter, a nickel, and a dime. He zipped shut the pocket. "Your change, sir. Hope you enjoy your postcards."

I thought for a moment, then said, "Twenty-five cents for the colored one and fifteen cents for the black and white make forty cents. You're charging me ten cents extra for each card."

He switched on his icy stare. "The prices I quoted to you earlier were Ermine Bandicoot's prices. I have to make a profit too, you know!" He had a way of shrieking when challenged which caused embarrassment. People would turn and stare —not at him, but at me!

"I see," said I. "Please get on with your story."

"Where was I?" he asked.

"I think you'd better get the cigarette rolled," I offered.

"Oh, yes, sure, of course. Ermine Bandicoot was at his best, rolling the cigarette. His collection at the time filled his closet, the maid's quarters, a tool shed, two whole silos and half another one. He had the butts for the job, and they were all fatties, no flatties—"

"What's a fatty and what's a flatty?" I interrupted.

"Fatties are full, round butts. Flatties are butts which have been put out by stepping on them. At first he collected both, but he soon weeded out the flatties. They're ugly."

"Such good taste," I muttered.

"What?"

"Oh, nothing. Go on with your story."

"The Statue of Liberty is one hundred and fifty-one feet tall, and its pedestal is one hundred and forty-two feet tall. That makes a total height of two hundred and ninety-three feet. He planned to make his cigarette three hundred feet tall so that it would top the tip of the Statue's torch by seven feet—"

"Great Scott," I gasped, "that's the length of a football field."

"Funny you should say that. We rolled it on our school field. The ten-yard markers were great for spreading the kids out evenly, four or so every ten yards, each kid with his bucket of wallpaper glue and brush. For a long time Ermine Bandicoot wondered what to use for cigarette paper; then he chose newsprint. That's the paper on which newspapers are printed. You must have seen rolls of newsprint on the backs of trucks. They're huge, very wide, and miles long. The kids spliced several overlapping strips with their glue pots, each kid wetting down two or three yards, all of them together lifting another strip of paper over the wet glue, then all together patting the strips neatly in place. Ermine Bandicoot ran up and down ·the field, directing and shouting orders like a drill sergeant. He must have covered quite a few miles, and—"

"Excuse me for interrupting again, but how did he get the kids to help him?"

"The kids were all in his little notebooks. They owed half-hours of work as interest for borrowing money, remember?"

"Oh, I see, those kids."

"Yes, those kids. Then came the big goof."

"What was that?"

"A magazine. Ermine Bandicoot asked a news magazine if it would like to photograph the rolling of the biggest cigarette in the history of the world. They said perhaps. They weren't excited. They imagined that the biggest cigarette in history wouldn't have to be over two feet long—not too exciting a news story. He told them it would be taller than the Statue of Liberty. They flipped. He asked them how much the story would be worth to them. They asked him what he wanted. He answered that he didn't want money, just to have the magazine move his butts from the farm to the football field, and furnish fifty buckets of wallpaper glue and fifty brushes, and rolls of newsprint. This seemed fair enough to them. A date was set. Now here comes the big goof. On the big day, four of the magazine's photographers arrived, strapped down with great equipment. The kids flipped. They work like beavers, screaming and hamming it up for the cameras. Ermine Bandicoot could have charged each kid fifty cents to roll that cigarette! Instead of which he scratched off all the debts in his books! A DUMB GOOF!" the kid barked. He stamped his foot with rage.

"How did the cigarette hold together?" I asked. "It would seem to me the butts would just fall out of the ends. Did he strip the butts?"

"What does 'strip the butts' mean?" He was still angry, and he didn't seem to want me to know anything about cigarettes that he didn't know.

"That's soldier talk for separating the paper from the tobacco."

"No, we didn't do that. We just piled them on the newsprint as they were. They didn't fall out of the ends because of filters. Ermine Bandicoot made two huge filters from cardboard cylinders. They were stuffed with cotton wadding and real fat hunks of charcoal, and painted to look just like cork.

"Why two?" I asked.

"So that the cigarette would hold together until stood on end. Once on end, held fast by guy wires, like a factory smokestack, the upper filter would be sliced off. The whole thing worked out beautifully, all fifty kids piling on butts, raking them, cameras clicking, Bandicoot screaming, all together rolling, all together pasting the final seam, patting it down, rolling the cigarette back and forth to

"... cameras clicking, Bandicoot screaming, all together rolling ..."

make it even." The kid jumped to his feet and held out his hand. "Sure could use another pop—throat's parched."

"What about the postcard money?" I asked impatiently.

"Can't touch it."

"Why not?"

"Do you think this is pleasure?" he shouted. "This is business!" It was another of his explosive outbursts. I found myself scrambling for change. He sprinted off to the square snack bar.

It seemed to me his story was falling apart. How would one move a hundred-yard-long cigarette—longer with the extra charcoal filter—through the streets? No double trailer truck would be long enough. It certainly couldn't turn street corners. It would be too fragile to stand much handling with derricks, too tall to balance on end. I asked for an explanation when he returned, slurping his big unknown-brand-pop bottle.

"Why do you want to know that?" said he, answering my question with another. He seemed bothered. He looked off to see how close we were to the docking berth.

"It would be too big to move anywhere. Even on wheels, it couldn't bend around corners."

"Oh, that," said the kid. His weasel eyes started

40

darting around. "The cigarette company used helicopters—yes, helicopters, one attached to each filter." A calmer expression returned to his face, and he was once again off and talking. "They used two huge canvas slings, like the bellybands which are put around elephants when they are hoisted aboard freighters." That latest idea made him smile. "The cigarette company wanted drama. 'We want drama!' they shouted. Helicopters were used"—he burst into giggles—"with elephant bellybands."

I noticed him looking forward more and more frequently, to see how close we were to docking. There was a sudden trembling and rumbling of engines, and the sound of water being thrashed and splashed. The ferryboat was being put in reverse, to slow her down for berthing. The action was a signal for passengers to jump up and parade past us, all rushing for a rapid exit.

"Let's get that tobacco in the harbor," said I.

"Oh, of course, sir, of course," said the kid, smiling. The "sir" and the smile came as a surprise —somewhat like a sullen, rotten waiter who turns all grins and kindness, starts whacking crumbs off the table—then presents the customer with his bill. He put his hands on my arm, as though to hold me down, gently, as he finished his tale. "The cigarette was stood on end, in place, by two ace

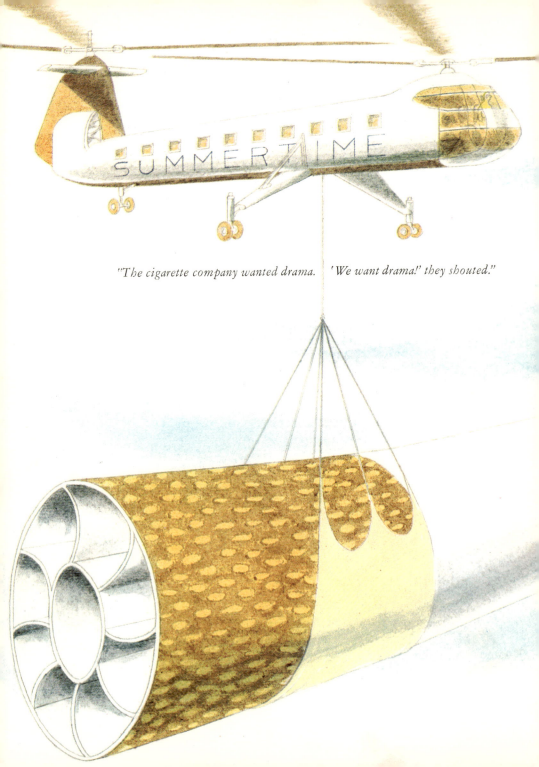

"The cigarette company wanted drama. 'We want drama!' they shouted."

helicopter pilots. There was one terrible moment when the cigarette slipped and buckled nearly in two, but it somehow held together. Ground crews fastened the guy wires. The upper filter was cleanly removed, and the tobacco trimmed by professional hedge-clippers.

"The first of the three days belonged entirely to the cigarette company. They erected a neon sign of the brand name, *Summertime*, which blinked on and off, up the front of the cigarette. They went so far as to replace the lights in the Statue of Liberty's torch with flickering bulbs, making her look indeed like a cigarette lighter, tall as a mountain. They were happy and proud. It looked great!

"The second day was all the Mayor's. Perched on a ladder, atop a whopping piece of fire-fighting equipment, he struck a match as big as a torch and lit the cigarette. His speech was short and to the point. 'Air pollution and cigarette smoking,' said he, 'ruin lungs and destroy health. With an aim to putting an end to both, I hereby light this horrible cigarette, with the single thought in mind of rousing the public's concern and anger against these menaces to city life and our very survival.' That was all. The Mayor seemed in a hurry to get down off that ladder.

"The cigarette burned calmly and correctly the

44

second night, and by morning it was one-fifth gone, about down to the Statue of Liberty's upraised elbow. It had a clean blue-gray ash on top. Its foul smoke—the smoke of a burning butt—rose high in the sky, thinned, and scattered.

"Then a fresh wind from the sea blew right up the harbor, into lower Manhattan. The terrible poisonous smoke from the monster butt invaded the downtown business section. Coughing broke out like the plague. The stock exchange closed in panic, choked out of action. The ghastly smoke crept uptown like a dragon, snarling traffic as people scrambled out of buildings, gasping for fresh air, clogging the streets—people bent double, scarlet-faced, tears coursing down hot cheeks.

"Meanwhile, the giant cigarette's brand name flashed merrily on and off—SUMMERTIME, SUMMERTIME, SUMMERTIME—for all within miles to see. An emergency meeting was called in the board room of the cigarette-company's offices. Flushed from choking, beet-red with rage, the president croaked, 'Who lit that damned cigarette?'

" 'Why, the Mayor, sir.'

" 'Great heavens, why?'

" 'We have no idea, sir.'

" 'It's SABOTAGE!'

" 'Yes, sir.'

" 'Shove it in the harbor. ON THE DOUBLE!'

" 'Yes, sir.'

"Less than an hour later, the guy wires on the Brooklyn side of the cigarette were cut. Like a burning tower of Pisa, the cigarette hesitated a long time before it slowly belly-flopped into the harbor off Bedloe's Island. There, with a great and horrible sizzling stink, it went out. Its many-layered newsprint paper slowly turned a cigar-brown. The Leviathan of cigarettes floated north toward downtown New York City, but soon slithered apart as the gooey, nicotine-poisoned wallpaper glue let go. A dirty brown dye spread slowly over the water, and Ermine Bandicoot's collection disintegrated, butt by butt, slowly thickening the harbor. And that, kind sir, is how Ermine Bandicoot fouled up New York harbor with cigarette tobacco."

The kid stood up, put one hand on his stomach, the other behind his back, and bowed.

"I believe, my dear sir, that we have arrived." This announcement was accompanied by jolting bumps, as the ferryboat bounced against the old, squeaking, groaning wooden pilings of its berth to a chain-rattling stop—then relative quiet. "I do hope," the kid went on, "that you've enjoyed your story half as much as I've enjoyed telling it to you."

I stupidly mumbled a few grunts.

46

"Sir, here is my card." He shoved a card deep in my jacket breast pocket. He was a mile of smiles. "You'll find it has my name, address, and telephone number. Get in touch with me if ever you should require my services for parties, luncheons, social gatherings, or whatever occasion."

He was standing square in front of me, with an upright palm outstretched. I found myself tipping him a dollar before I could think what I was doing. Besides, he seemed to be barring the passage between me and the exit, and the ship's crew were urging us off the boat hurriedly. He grabbed the dollar, sprinted for shore like a gazelle, and was out of sight in seconds.

I had come to Staten Island to see an exhibition of paintings. My father, a painter, had spent a good many years of his life living on Staten Island. The art museum was having a show of several of his landscapes, most of which had been painted on the Island. I had been invited to the opening. I had a good lunch first, spent quite a good bit of time at the exhibition, then headed for the ferry which would take me home to New York City. As I boarded the boat, there was the kid again. His beady black eyes were positively spinning in his skinny head. He was scanning the passengers, looking, I supposed, for a victim such as I had been on our previous crossing. I wondered how he would act when he saw me again. Our eyes met. He did nothing, just looked right through me. I sat down on a long bench on deck to watch his performance.

A pleasant-looking gentleman then descended the ramp and boarded the ferry. He was wearing a green tweed suit, tweed cap, and though the afternoon sun was still shining through cotton wisps of clouds, carrying an umbrella. I could tell by the man's excitement in his surroundings that he was a visitor, not a regular commuter. I guessed him to be a middle-class Englishman. Poor Englishmen usually have but one suit, a dark one, and usually wear working clothes. Rich Englishmen rarely wear green suits. Middle-class Englishmen have two suits, one dark for the city, one green for the country—tidy thinking, based, I imagine, on the animal laws of camouflage. The man walked forward, leaned on the rail, and intently studied that touristic sight of sights, the lower-Manhattan skyline.

As can be seen, I'd temporarily taken my eyes off the kid with the ratlike face. I quickly looked for him, and, sure enough, he too had spotted our man in green from Britain. "Oh, no," I said aloud to myself. Too late. The kid's face was just to starboard of the Englishman's, a bit lower than his right ear. The kid too leaned on the rail and looked at the skyscrapers, the wheels of his conniving brain turning full-throttle. He was looking back and forth from Englishman's ear to skyscrapers, Englishman's ear to skyscrapers. He coughed, then made his opening statement. I was just a bit too far away to overhear what he said, but the Englishman turned to the kid, straightened up tall, umbrella at his side like a saber, and made a thundering *HARRUMPH!* sound. He then spun around full-turn, presenting his back to the kid, and marched off in splendid military fashion.

Britishers enjoy their privacy more than any other people in the world. The sassy miser had bumped up against a solid stone wall. I headed for the snack bar to celebrate with a hot dog and coke —not too grand, but best on hand. At least I wouldn't be paying for two this trip.

. . . and made a thundering HARRUMPH! sound.

I proceeded to add up in my mind what the tale of how Ermine Bandicoot flecked New York harbor with tobacco had cost me in cold cash:

hot dog and soda pop	55¢
another hot dog	30¢
apple turnover, ice cream,	
and soda pop	75¢
candy bars	55¢
postcards	60¢
still another soda pop	25¢
tip	1.00
total	$4.00

I was interrupted in my thoughts by great bursts of British laughter, approaching me from behind. Before I could turn, one of the ladies behind the snack bar jabbed another with her elbow and muttered, "The weasel's caught another fish." I spun around, and there, red-faced with laughter, was the man in the green tweed suit.

"Ermine Bandicoot!" he shouted. "You cannot make me believe that anyone could have such a silly name."

"But it's true, sir," said the kid, "and as I said, Ermine Bandicoot is without doubt one of the brightest young internationalists of this or any other year."

"Tell me more about him later," said the Britisher. "But first, what is that 'very-American' drink you insist that I try?"

"Root beer," said the kid.

"Heavens, sounds awful! What the devil is it made of?"

"Roots," the kid answered, "all kinds of juicy roots. Give us two root beers," he ordered, "and your two longest hot dogs, piled high with all the goodies. And make 'em hot and spicy; this is a distinguished guest," he added, bowing to the man in green, "a distinguished guest from fair and distant shores."

The word *guest* seemed to have slipped loosely from his mouth, for when the lady at the counter said, "That will be one dollar and ten cents, please," the kid's attention was found to be riveted on some fascinating object way off on the horizon. The "guest" found himself fumbling uneasily through a palm full of American coins which he hadn't, as yet, quite learned to understand.

"Thank you very much, sir," the kid said, upon awakening from his daydream. "Yes, as I was saying out on deck, Ermine Bandicoot's idea, the Cosa Nostril, is the best-ever peace plan for a sorely troubled world, and—"

"But isn't the Cosa Nostra an organization of

gangsters and racketeers?" the man in the green suit interrupted.

"The Cosa Nostra is exactly that. Yes," answered the kid, " 'Cosa' means thing, 'Nostra' means our, our thing—a sort of Robin Hood one-for-all-and-all-for-one idea, one terrible, evil family of hoods, crooks, and murderers. Now the Cosa Nostril is something else again. 'Cosa' means thing, 'Nostril' means nose—more or less—and there you have the Nose Thing. Now out on deck you were looking for the United Nations building, and you said that it looked like a giant filing cabinet. I quite agree. That was brilliant. I might use that remark in the future—if you don't mind, sir. The United Nations is too complicated. One huge filing cabinet, stuffed with too many bits and scraps of paper, too many voices, too many nations. Now Ermine Bandicoot, whose powers of observation are nearly as sharp and shiny as your own, sir, noticed that most of the world leaders worth their salt have big noses. A big nose is a source of joy and comfort to everyone. The Cosa Nostril would have as members the super-beaks of the world, ex-President Lyndon Johnson of America, Prime Minister Indira Gandhi of India, big Charles de Gaulle of France, Prime Minister Golda Meir of Israel, President Abdel Nasser of Egypt, among others.

53

"The Cosa Nostril would meet at least twice a year to clear the air, release tensions. The world would breathe easier, thanks to the Cosa Nostril. As a matter of fact, Ermine Bandicoot's motto for the Cosa Nostril is 'Breathe easier through us!' Brilliant, what? Makes one feel good all over."

"What an amazing young chap!" said the Britisher.

"Ermine Bandicoot's brain is a gift to mankind," the kid continued. "Come on, let's get out in the fresh air." He gave me a snotty look. He apparently didn't like giving anything away, not even free stories. They wandered off, on deck.

For no reason that I can remember, I suddenly plunged my fingers into my breast pocket and pulled out the kid's card. It was handmade. It had neat tiny letters, perhaps written with a crow-quill pen and India ink, on a cut-up piece of bristol board. It read:

ERMINE BANDICOOT

STORIES AND INVENTIONS
ANY SUBJECT MATTER
ENTERTAINMENT GUARANTEED

And then it gave the address and telephone number of the YMCA Club where he lived and could be reached.

I next looked at the postcards. They were cruder than the handmade visiting card, just cheap commercial cards of the Statue of Liberty, with a hand-painted cigarette next to it, sloppily drawn. I wandered out on deck, perhaps to get away from the snack bar smell, but more likely to eavesdrop on Ermine Bandicoot describing himself to the Englishman. I could overhear only snatches of conversation because upon seeing me approaching, he would dummy up at once.

On one trip around the deck he was saying, "If tiny little Cub Scouts can start a fire by rubbing two sticks together, just imagine the warmth of goodwill which would radiate throughout the world from Cosa Nostril Eskimo kisses." The Englishman appeared to be charmed. He was beaming with contentment. I wondered if I had looked that hypnotized upon hearing my story.

I thought again of that cigarette. If it were to be in the right proportion and was three hundred feet long, it would have to have a diameter of at least thirty-three feet. No number of boys could roll such a cigarette, no layers of newsprint could hold it together, and no one Ermine Bandicoot could collect enough butts to fill it if he devoted his entire lifetime to the job. Then I thought further that no two helicopters in the world today could lift it, and no elephants are fat enough around the middle to require bellybands which could encircle such a monstrous thing. As I came around deck again, the two had left. I looked inside and there they were. The kid was eating an apple turnover and ice cream and drinking more root beer.

I wondered if he made up stories as he went along or if he had a collection of stories to fit any occasion. He saw me looking at the water and told me "How Ermine Bandicoot Filled New York Harbor with Cigarette Tobacco." When he first saw the Englishman, he tried to figure out where he was looking. His first guess was a mistake. He was given a brusque brush-off. Not giving up that easily, he had tried "Ermine Bandicoot and the Cosa Nostril" and had scored a bull's-eye. The Englishman had obviously been scanning the sky-line, looking for the United Nations building. The kid probably had other stories to tell, stored away, more or less polished, ready to roll, such as "Ermine Bandicoot, Human Fly," "Ermine Bandicoot's Escapes in New York Harbor Top Houdini's," "Ermine Bandicoot's Death Leap from the Verrazano Bridge," "Ermine Bandicoot Puts an End to Polo on Governor's Island," "Ermine Bandicoot's Plan for Ellis Island." I was only guessing, but he seemed to operate that way—pick his man, guess his interest, sock him with a punchy opening line, then weasel food, drink, and money out of him.

I wondered if he had postcards to go with every story. How could he match the Cosa Nostril with an appropriate postcard? How could he fake a picture of Charles de Gaulle and Indira Gandhi rubbing noses Eskimo-style? Or Abdel and Golda? Or Lyndon and Indira? Or a group photo of the lot wearing fezzes, twenty-gallon Stetsons, Generals' caps—all laughing it up for peace?

Of course I underestimated him.

As I rounded the deck again, they were back outside.

"Have you seen Pablo Picasso's famous painting of the white dove of peace?" the kid was asking.

"Yes, I have," the man in the green suit replied.

"And you've probably noticed that Pablo Picasso, in addition to having piercing eyes, like marbles, is also gifted with an outsized schnozzola?"

"It hadn't occurred to me, but I guess you're right," said the Englishman.

"Well, Ermine Bandicoot wrote Picasso and, using famous big noses as bait, persuaded the master to paint a new, big-beaked, white dove of peace just for the Cosa Nostril."

"Fine thinking," the Englishman said. "How bright and witty."

57

"Color postcards were made of the painting," the kid continued, "and I just happen to have a few on me." He flew a card of a dove past the Britisher's eyes. "Would you care for some? They're only fifty cents apiece."

The man in the green suit winced, coughed. "I guess I'll take a couple," he said. He held out his fistful of unfamiliar American coins—a much-smaller fistful than I'd seen earlier at the snack bar.

The kid poked through it, counting out loud as he added up to a dollar. He zipped the dollar in one of his pockets, shoved the postcards in another brown envelope, sealed it up tight, and handed it to the Britisher. "Enjoy them, sir," said he.

"Why, yes," said the poor chap. He looked about him with some embarrassment, hoping he hadn't been caught doing something silly.

What a rascal that kid was! All he had done, of course, was to buy a bunch of Picasso peace-dove postcards at the United Nations building, take them home, and fatten and lengthen the dove's nose with white poster paint.

After we had docked, the kid pulled the same trick on the Englishman as he had on me, blocking his passage off the boat with an outstretched palm. The poor Englishman again fished for his fistful of coins and gave the kid the lot.

58

. . . blocking his passage off the boat with an outstretched palm.

"Thank you very much, sir. Hope you enjoy your postcards, sir. Have a good stay in America, and please, sir, spread the good word about Ermine Bandicoot and the Cosa Nostril when you are safely back in fair England." The kid bowed and bolted for shore, only this time I raced after him.

Once out of the Englishman's sight, the kid slowed down and shuddered violently, as though the whole episode had been an unpleasant experience. He then shrugged his skinny shoulders, shoved his hands deep in the pockets of his buttoned-down suit, and walked off, down the gutters of lower Manhattan. He was kicking trash, looking for lost coins and, in this sad pursuit, made a pathetic silhouette. I spotted a whole unsmoked cigarette in his path ahead. I wondered what he would do about it. It stopped him cold. He seemed about to pounce on it when he suddenly straightened up and with his pointed shoe, ferociously ground it from fatty to flatty. He grunted and walked on.

Then an extraordinary thing happened.

A Rolls-Royce limousine drove up alongside him. It was chauffeur driven, shiny-black and bulgy. It had tiny blue cut-glass carriage lamps, and a fat flexible telephone aerial, which was gently whipping the evening air. The car didn't make a sound. A rear window opened and a thin pale hand holding a fat envelope jutted out. A precise voice said, "Hermann, your mother and I would *very much* like you to come home."

The kid went on kicking trash, giving the gutter his full attention.

"Hermann, your mother would like you to take this." He limply waved the fat envelope.

The kid didn't even look up.

The pale waving hand followed the kid along for the length of a block, then the hand and its envelope withdrew. The Rolls-Royce sped away.

"Who was that?" I rudely asked a uniformed doorman.

"That's old Hermann Vanden Kroote," he answered, "and the skinny nut in the gutter is Hermann Vanden Kroote, Jr."

"Does the father sell munitions?"

"Heck no," said the doorman, "cigarettes. You know, *Summertime* regulars and *Wintertime* menthols. *Mayfair Lady* extra mild, and *Copper Goddess* pipe tobacco. He owns that huge Vanden Kroote building overlooking the harbor. That nut son of his won't take a nickel of his money, says he's selling sickness. Well, one of them is *really* sick, and it sure ain't old Pop. The young punks of today—"

The kid walked on his lonely way.

"Thank you," said I, rushing off after the kid. It occurred to me that he was existing on rotten snack-bar food and might like a real meal.

"Hey, Bandicoot!" I shouted.

The kid stopped short in his tracks, as though struck by a dart in the middle of the back. He slowly turned and looked at me. "Oh, it's you," said he. "Now what?"

"How about having dinner with me?"

"I don't accept charity." He turned his back. "I'm talked out for today."

"Sorry I asked," said I.

The kid walked on his lonely way.

Ermine Bandicoot was as great as he said he was.

It's tough to be a kid and have principles. It's really tough to squeeze out a miserly existence, going to and from school, particularly if you happen to choose that oldest of noble professions, storytelling.